Little Tom Turkey

BY

FRANCES BLOXAM

ILLUSTRATED BY

JIM SOLLERS

DOWN EAST BOOKS

With thanks to all the friends and members
of the Southgate Sportsman's Club who shared
turkey stories and lore; special thanks to
Brad Mallett, Maine guide and turkey expert,
who generously gave help and information.
And thanks to Big Dog for the inspiration.

· F. B. ·

To Loren, Carol, Harold, Janet, and Melody.

· J. S. ·

STORY © 2005 BY FRANCES BLOXAM.
ILLUSTRATIONS © 2005 BY JAMES SOLLERS.
ALL RIGHTS RESERVED.
ISBN: 0-89272-671-7
LCCN: 2004112594
DESIGN BY LURELLE CHEVERIE
PRINTED IN CHINA RPS

5 4 3 2 1

DOWN EAST BOOKS
A DIVISION OF DOWN EAST ENTERPRISE, INC.
PUBLISHER OF DOWN EAST, THE MAGAZINE OF MAINE

BOOK ORDERS: 1-800-685-7962
WWW.DOWNEASTBOOKS.COM

When little Tom hatched from a beautiful egg,
the first thing he saw was his mother's long leg.

He came out of his shell quite soggy and wet.
What would he look like? You couldn't tell yet.

Hen turkey settled
back down on her nest
and cuddled her hatchlings
close to her breast.

Mother hen's feathers were fluffy and soft,
so Tom snoozed for a bit while his feathers dried off.

There were nine older hatchlings close to the nest.
Little Tom wobbled out and stood with the rest.

Mother Hen called them and said to her brood
"Now, you all need a lesson in how to get food.

Watch what I do and scratch with your feet.
You'll find some nice bugs and seeds you can eat!

Scratch, little turkeys, and look for a treat!"
Tom scratched—and it felt really good to his feet.

It took a few tries
   to get things just right
but soon he was scratching
   from morning till night.

So then he ate bugs and
   seeds with such vigor
it filled him right up and
   made him grow bigger!

The hen took the flock to the edge of the wood.
Close to the meadow, she stopped and she stood.

Little Tom looked ahead and in front of his eyes
was a marvelous turkey of remarkable size.

His feathers just glistened and shone in the light.
Never had little Tom seen such a sight.

His elegant head was red, white, and blue.
This bird had a beard and handsome spurs, too.

Then Big Gobbler did what a gobbler does best.
He pulled back his head and puffed out his chest.

He fanned out his tail and slow-marched with his feet . . .
and strutted right by without missing a beat.

A wonderful gobbler! A turkey supreme!
To strut just like him was little Tom's dream!

"Oh, how I would love
    to do that same thing—
to fluff out my feathers
    and strut like a king!"

So then little Tom
    stretched up quite tall
and tried hard to strut,
    but he still was too small.

His balance was off.
    He tripped over his feet.
His tail was too short
    —and he fell on his beak.

The hen called her little poults back to her side and gave them some lessons on how to survive.

"You must be wary. You must be fast.
You must watch out if you're going to last!

Beware of coyotes. Beware of the fox!
Enemies lurk behind trees and big rocks!

Now, flap your wings and try hard to fly—
flying decides if you live or you die!"

Everyone flapped, but no one took off.
They were too young, with wing feathers too soft.

All through the summer,
as he ate and he grew

Tom practiced his flying
and tried strutting, too.

He'd pull back his head,
but his chest wouldn't puff
and his tail wouldn't spread—
it really was tough.

On a day when the flock
was pecking and scratching,
they all felt quite safe,
but *someone was watching!*

A fox, who was hungry, thought they would taste good.
He crept slowly forward, out of the wood.

"Run little ones! There's a fox over there!
Run as fast as you can! There's no time to spare!"

All the poults ran as fast as they could.
They hoped to be safe in the midst of the wood.

The fox was so close that Tom plainly could hear
the snap of fox jaws right on his rear!

"I'd better get going, or I have a hunch
I could end the day as this red fellow's lunch!"

Tom ran, but the fox was right on his tail!

Tom gave a big leap—and he started to sail!

His wings really worked! He had power to spare.
What a wonderful feeling to soar through the air!

Tom's landing was off,
too much wobble and flutter.
"But I got away, and
     next time I'll do better.

"Now that I'm flying, perhaps it is true
that I'm ready for strutting—I'll try that out too!"

Once again little Tom tried out his strut,
hoping this time *not* to fall on his butt.

He fluffed up his feathers
    and threw out his chest.
He flopped down his wings
    and gave it his best.
He spread out his tail,
    got his legs into gear—

but, alas! He still ended up on his rear.

Then winter came. The meadows were brown.
The flock searched for food and the snow drifted down.

The winter was cold and the winter was long.
Though he didn't know it, young Tom had grown strong.

Winter *did* end, and the meadow turned green—
the bugs, leaves, and berries were once again seen.

One warm spring morning, young Tom flew down
from his roost in a tree to sunbathe on the ground.

He went to the brook and bent over to drink.
What he saw in the water caused him to blink!

He stood there amazed at the turkey reflected;
the image he saw was *not* what he expected.

No more little Tom—now a gobbler of size!
The way he had changed came as quite a surprise!

His feathers just glistened, there were spurs on his feet
and he had a beard—he was gobbler, complete!

His elegant head was red, white, and blue.
He was totally gobbler, handsome and new!

The new gobbler did
　　what a gobbler does best.
He pulled back his head
　　and puffed out his chest.

He fanned out his tail and
　　slow-marched with his feet
and strutted right by
　　without missing a beat.

He strutted a strut
　　that was fit for a king!
A strut of perfection
　　of head, tail, and wing.

O, wonderful gobbler! O, turkey supreme!

At last young Tom turkey was living his dream.

LET'S TALK ABOUT WILD TURKEYS . . .

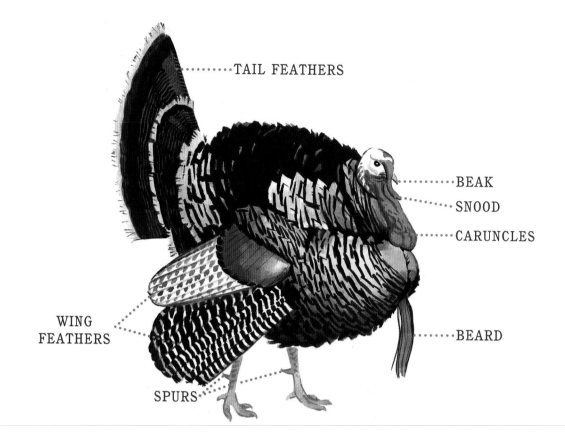

TAIL FEATHERS

BEAK

SNOOD

CARUNCLES

WING FEATHERS

BEARD

SPURS

FULL-GROWN MALE
(GOBBLER or TOM)

Where do wild turkeys live?
And sleep? And eat?

Wild turkeys live in forests, fields, and meadows. They need trees for nuts and fruits, bushes for berries, and sunny edges of fields for insects, grain, and seeds. They also need a stream, river, or pond nearby for water. They roost (sleep) in the forest trees.

Does a flock stay in
one place all the time?

No, they move as needed for food. Turkeys eat a great deal, so once they have eaten everything they like in one location, they move on.

Are wild turkeys like the domestic turkeys on farms?

No, they are quite different. Wild turkeys are taller and have long, powerful legs, longer necks, and great, strong wings. They are stream-lined. Farm turkeys are bred to be heavy and meaty, with plump legs and breasts. Wild turkeys are strong, fast fliers (up to fifty-five miles per hour!), while domestic turkeys have smaller wings and quickly grow too big and heavy to fly at all.

Do wild turkeys lay eggs every day the way chickens do?

No, a hen turkey will lay eggs only in the spring, sometime in February, March, or April, depending on where she lives. She will lay one nearly every day until there are ten or twelve. Her "nest" is just a shallow depression in the earth, where the eggs will be hard to spot. She also covers them with leaves. When she is done laying, she sits on the eggs to keep them warm so they will hatch.

What does a hen turkey do to protect her eggs?

If there is a predator around who likes to eat eggs (such as a fox, skunk, raccoon or weasel), the hen sits absolutely still. If this doesn't work and the animal finds her, she will run from the nest and finally fly away to escape. She will return if the eggs are still there.

FEMALE
(HEN)

How long does it take for the eggs to hatch?

It takes twenty-six to twenty-eight days. The poults are strong enough to leave the nest to look for food when they are less than a day old. Poults eat insects, seeds, and berries. As they get older they will eat nuts, grain, fruits, and just about anything else!

If I see a wild turkey, how can I tell if it is a hen or a tom?

A tom turkey is a large, handsome bird with a featherless, colorful head, spurs on his legs, and a "beard" sprouting from his chest. His feathers are iridescent, and he is a fine sight. A hen is smaller. She has no spurs or beard, and her head has a few feathers. Her general appearance is very drab. She needs this lack of color to make her hard to see; this keeps her and her brood safe.

YOUNG MALE
(JAKE)

Do all turkeys strut?

No, only toms strut, and they do it mostly in the spring. The strut is a courtship action the toms use to show off for the hens. Toms may strut so often and enthusiastically that they wear off the tips of their wing feathers!

LOOK FOR TURKEYS BY COUNTRY ROADS AND FIELDS IN THE SPRING, WHEN THEY ARE MOVING THE MOST. LOOK HARD—THEY'RE NOT EASY TO SEE!